The Adventures of JJ
at the Double J Ranch

Written and Illustrated by Fawn Williams

PublishAmerica
Baltimore

First printing

ISBN: 9781462642519
PUBLISHED BY PUBLISHAMERICA, LLLP
www.publishamerica.com
Baltimore

Printed in the United States of America

This book is dedicated to my husband, Charles A. Kennedy.
Thank you for being there for me.
And to my mom, I love you.
And to Amanda Stinnett.

Hi, I am JJ.

Today I would like to take you on an adventure to the Double J Ranch.

The Double J Ranch is a working horse ranch that has a lot of horses.

They raise, train and sell Tennessee Walking Horses.

A Tennessee Walking horse is a breed of horse that is gaited. Gaited is a manner of walking or running. But first I think we need to go shopping for some things.

When I arrived at the store, a man by the name of Ben came over to me to see what I needed.

I told him that I would like to buy a cowboy hat, and cowboy boots. And I asked him is he had a cowboy hat and cowboy boots in my size.

He told me that the thought he had my size.

So first we went to the hats.
The first one was too big.
The second one was too small.
But the third one fit just right.

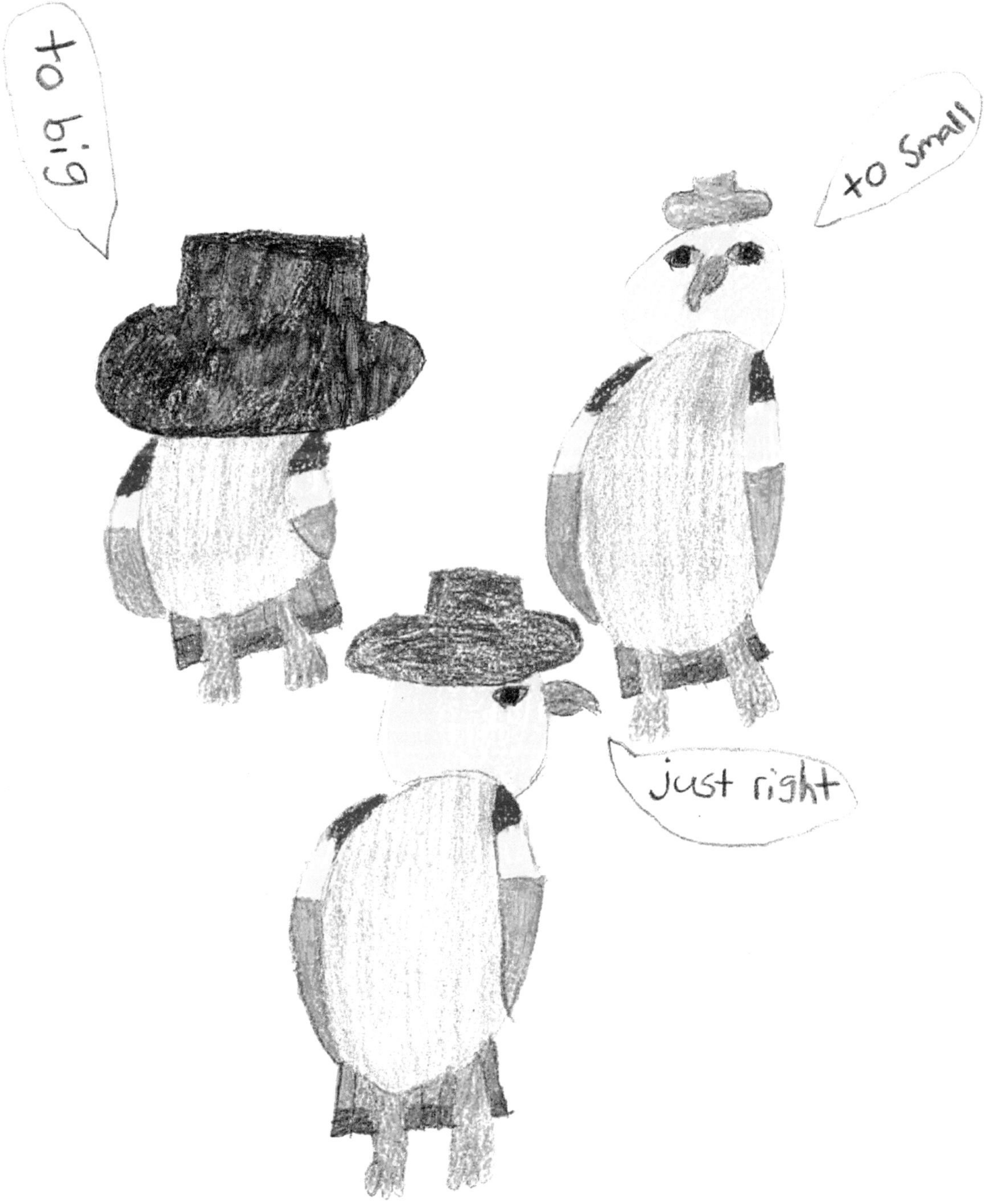
to big
to Small
just right

Next we went to the boots.

The first one was too small.

The second one was too big.

But the third one fit just right.

Now that we have our hats and boots, we can go to the Double J Ranch.

At the ranch Fawn and Red was there to welcome me to the horse ranch. Fawn told me that the first thing we need to do is feed and water the horses. She said that two times a day we feed the horses and that each horse gets 20 pounds of hay a day.

Next she told me that we need to clean the stable and put in new bedding.

As we were cleaning out the stable, Fawn and Red got a very important phone call from their vet.

He told them that one of your neighbor's horses are being quarantined because of a deadly disease.

And that you need to move your horses and vaccinate them.

Vaccinating is when a doctor gives you a shot so that you won't get sick.

After Fawn got off the phone, she told me that we need to move the horses from one pasture to another to be vaccinated from this deadly disease.

So we ran to the stable to tack up our horses for the long ride.

Tack up is when you put the bridle and saddle on your horse.

As we were mounting our horses, Fawn told us that it may take two days to get the horses to the pasture to get vaccinated.

As we were on our ride through the prairie, we could see the white tail deer eating some prairie grass off in the distance.

And the birds were signing, their beautiful songs.

As the day went on, I was thinking about what a beautiful day it was.

Till we came to a cliff with a steep drop.

We stop our horses.

As Red told me that if I look there in the distance, you can see the herd of horses.

As I was looking down the steep cliff, I asked Red, "How do we get down there?"

He told me that 20 miles north of here there is a trail that leads to the bottom.

When we got to the trail I did not think the horses could go down it.
There came to be a lot of big rocks on the trail.
But as we went on, I could see that it was no big deal.

When we got to the bottom of the trail we made our way to the herd of horses.

When we got to the horses, Fawn and Red told me that we will camp here.

And tomorrow we will lead the horses up the steep cliff and to the pasture.

That night as we were sitting by the camp fire, Red and Fawn told about the good old days and how the ancestors, used to do this all the time.

They used to take the cows and horses from one pasture to another.

The next day we packed up camp, and mounted our horses and started on our way up the steep cliff with the herd of horses.

By the time we got to the pasture, the sun was almost down.

So the next day we started to vaccinated the horses.

It took us five days to give all the horses the vaccination.

And now you know what it is like to live and work on a horse ranch. I hope you had fun. I know I did, and until next time, bye.

The End

Would you like to see your manuscript become a book?

If you are interested in becoming a PublishAmerica author, please submit your manuscript for possible publication to us at:

acquisitions@publishamerica.com

You may also mail in your manuscript to:

**PublishAmerica
PO Box 151
Frederick, MD 21705**

www.publishamerica.com

Lightning Source UK Ltd.
Milton Keynes UK
UKRC01n2206020217
293497UK00004B/28

9 781462 645589